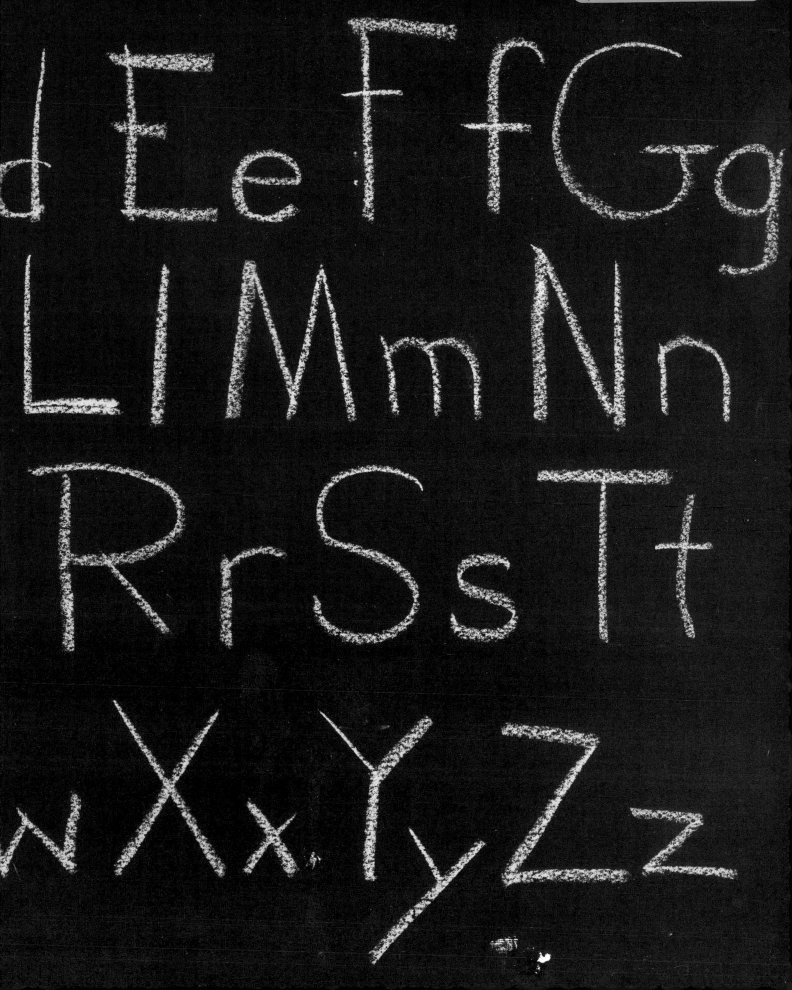

For Mother Margaret,
who opened her heart and let her stories fill mine
—L. C-R.

To my children—Jaime, Maya, Malcolm, Leila, and Nola
—J.R.

The Boston Post
The Thirteenth Amendment Ends Slavery

Freedom's School

by Lesa Cline-Ransome

Illustrations by James E. Ransome

 JUMP AT THE SUN

Los Angeles   New York

"We went to sleep slaves and woke up free," Mama told me and my little brother, Paul, the day freedom came. She looked at me and said, "Lizzie, bein' free means we got to work harder than ever before. And I don't just mean in the field. Real freedom means 'rithmetic and writing."

Just like the livestock gobbled up food scraps flung by the Master, Mama and Daddy had picked up scraps of learning at church. Preacher gave them pieces of words here and there. Every time Mama and Daddy got a piece, they'd give me and Paul some, too. But scraps of learning don't amount to much—they just made me hungry for more.

My mama and daddy'll have to work their crop alone, 'cause Mama made her mind up that me and Paul are going to that new school just for us.

"Everybody working in their own way, Lizzie," Daddy said.

I couldn't wait to get to work on my schooling.

'Fore me and Paul left for school that first morning, Mama told us, "Walk as fast as you can, and stay together."

We were not halfway there when we saw white folks along the road. Some said mean things.

"Where y'all in a hurry to?" I heard behind me as we passed a group of boys. I could feel the hate in their voices. I grabbed Paul's hand and walked faster. Not fast enough, 'cause one rock hit me on my leg and another hit my back.

I thought of Mama then. I didn't say nothing, but I turned, spit, and ran.

The schoolhouse hadn't been painted yet, and it was real plain looking, but I never seen a prettier sight.

Inside were long benches and tables of rough wood, lined up like rows of cotton. In the corner was a crooked fireplace. School smelled new, like fresh-cut wood. Raw and sweet.

In ones and twos and threes, kids came in and sat around us. Lena, Ruby, then Kat and Elbert. Knew some of them from church, some from the fields. Soon, the school was all filled up.

The teacher wrote on a board and said her name was Mizz Howard. Her skin was just as brown as mine, and her hair was pulled smooth in a bun. When she spoke, it was in smiles. She asked everyone their names. I kept my head down when I said "Lizzie," careful not to look in her eyes, so she'd know I was respectful. Then she started our first lesson.

Paul didn't know as many letters as me, so he looked to see what I was doing. Some kids weren't writing on their slates. Mizz Howard went over and put her hand on theirs to show them how to make letters. I put my hand on Paul's, and after he got the first couple, he shook my hand off and worked by himself. His letters didn't look like mine. They big and wiggly, but he was proud just the same.

The walk home felt longer than the walk coming. We got home in time for Paul to fetch water and get the fire going. I mixed the meal for cornbread and made a little bit of greens with the last piece of salt pork. Our mama and daddy were so tired when they got in from the fields, they didn't even seem hungry.

'Fore we went to bed, me and Paul copied our letters at the table. Mama braided my hair, and Daddy sat across from us, sharpening a tool. We had to answer so many of Mama's questions, it was hard to get our practicing done.

"How many folks showed up?" and "Is the learnin' hard?" Even questions about the new teacher. "What kind of dress she wear?"

Some days when we got to school, there were lots of seats empty. At harvest time, families needed the extra help to get the crop in. Most of the bigger boys were gone. Lest it rained, we probably wouldn't see them again till winter. I felt sorry for them. It was hard enough to keep up with school, let alone try and catch up on something you never learned.

Once we had to turn right around and go back home, 'cause Mizz Howard said it wasn't safe to be at school that day. But Paul always needs answers, so he marched right up to her and asked, "Why can't we stay at school, Teacher?"

"Just run on home now, Paul, and I'll see you tomorrow," she said. I don't think she wanted us to see the frown behind her smile.

In winter, walking to school got harder. The wind whipped our faces as soon as we stepped out the door, and it never let up. Paul had to wear some of Pa's old boots, but they so big, it sounded like he was marching when he walked. Cold weather kept some kids home. I told Paul the white schools got a stove to keep them warm in the winter. Not a fireplace with more wind blowing in than heat coming out.

"Why do white folks get so mad over us getting something they already got?" he asked.

I didn't have an answer.

Sometimes Mizz Howard had me read to some of the younger kids. There just wasn't enough of her to go around. I liked to pretend I was the teacher and this was my class.

One day, there was a pounding at the door, and we all looked up from our work. The room went quiet, and for a moment Mizz Howard didn't move. I wondered if it was some of those white folks. More pounding, and Mizz Howard wiped her hands on her dress. She tried on a smile and said, "Keep working, children."

Instead of working, we watched her walk toward the door.

Shadows and voices filled the doorway, and Mizz Howard disappeared into the cold. Through the window I saw our neighbor, Mr. Hodges, and his two big sons. They been working next to their daddy all their lives. Mr. Hodges's voice got louder. "Please, Teacher, work's been keepin' them in the fields, but if they can just sit in the back a spell, they could learn somethin'. And they can work. Help with anythin' you need 'round here."

"Ain't they too old?" Paul whispered to me.

They talked a little while longer, and when Mizz Howard came back, Mr. Hodges's boys were behind her, their feet cracked and dirty, their heads hanging down. They walked to the back of the class, not looking at anyone, and sat on the bench against the wall. As Teacher told us to take out our slates and practice our letters, I turned to them and smiled.

A few days later, we were almost at the school when we smelled the smoke. We ran the rest of the way, till we saw Mizz Howard.

"Why? Why? Why?" She was crying and shouting at the same time. She paced back and forth, staring at the flames.

Folks came from everywhere, fetching pails of water and throwing them onto our burning schoolhouse. But nothing would stop the fire from swallowing it up.

We were worn out and quiet on the walk home. Thinking about Mizz Howard, the fire, our school, took all the words from us.

When we got back, I ran into Mama's arms and let myself cry long and hard.

"At least they got a little learnin' 'fore the school burnt," Daddy said to Mama, I think to make us both feel better. Mama didn't answer, I didn't neither. 'Cause we both knew that halfway to freedom feels like no freedom at all.

Even though we didn't have a school, Mama told me to keep practicing. I read the two books Mizz Howard gave me, over and over, until I knew the words by heart. I read them to Paul and sometimes my mama, when she wasn't too tired to listen.

"Are we ever gonna go back to school?" I kept asking her. She would say, "Things take time, Lizzie. You got to be patient." I wonder if being patient means to just keep waiting till you don't want it no more.

On the first warm day, Mama woke us at dawn.

"Hurry, now. Get yourselves washed and dressed. We gonna walk over to that school and check on Mizz Howard. See how she's holdin' up," Mama said.

First we heard the hammering and sawing. Then we heard the voices, loud and laughing. Around the bend we saw Preacher, Mr. Hodges, and his boys, too. Looked like everybody brought whatever they had—wood, nails, saws. Paul and I ran ahead of Mama to see Mizz Howard. She was spreading a quilt on the grass in front of our burned-down school. A few of the spelling books were there, black around the edges, and a couple of slates, too.

"Paul, Lizzie, come and and join us. I am just getting ready to start today's lesson," she said, waving us over.

Behind Mizz Howard, where the old school was, we saw Daddy, standing tall and proud, a hammer in his hand.

When we hugged him, we breathed in the smell of fresh-cut wood. Raw and sweet.

"Daddy, you're helping build my school?" I asked.

"No, Lizzie, we're *all* helping to build Freedom's school."

First Edition
Printed in Malaysia

10 9 8 7 6 5 4 3 2 1

H106-9333-5-14258

Library of Congress Cataloging-in-Publication Data

Cline-Ransome, Lesa.
  Freedom's school / by Lesa Cline-Ransome ; illustrations by James E. Ransome.
      pages cm
  Summary: Hungry for learning, Lizzie and her brother Paul attend a new school built for
freed slaves.
  ISBN 978-1-4231-6103-5
[1. Education—Fiction. 2. Schools—Fiction. 3. Freedmen—Fiction. 4. African Americans—
Fiction.] I. Ransome, James, illustrator II. Title.
  PZ7.C622812Fr 2015
  [E]—dc23   2013013756

This book is set in Hoefler Text.
Designed by Tyler Nevins
Reinforced binding
Visit www.DisneyBooks.com

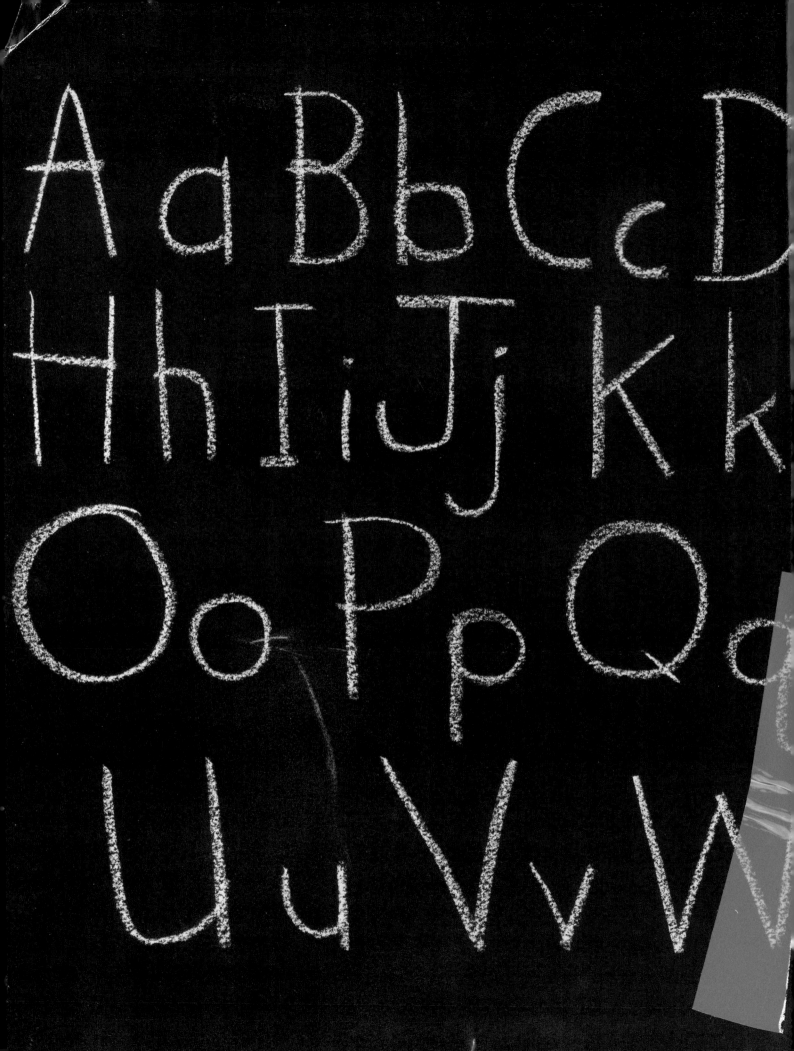